Noise
in the
Barn

Evelyn Heckhaus

To order additional copies of this book, contact:
Xlibris
1-888-795-4274
www.Xlibris.com
Orders@Xlibris.com

Dedicated
to my grandson Nathaniel,
who has a responsible and helping
attitude.

Noise in the Barn

"I sure do not look forward to cleaning the storage room at the barn", said Nat. "I'm thinking about those cobwebs and piles of leaves pushed up into the corner. I bet my goats have been in there, chewing and destroying stuff, too." His Saturday chore for this week had been on his chore list for several days.

"Maybe, cousin Alex will come over to help me", Nat said, "or distract me."

Nat was the neat one. His bedroom always had each toy properly placed on shelves. He was careful to store his freshly laundered clothes in his dresser. His bed linens were tucked in on all sides. His mom hoped he would use his organizational skills to improve the storage area in the barn.

"Hey, Alex, come on over," said Nat as he watched his cousin walking around in the yard next door.

"What are you going to do today, cousin?" asked cousin Alex who seldom had any chores assigned on Saturday.

"I'm working on the barn storage room – get out the cobwebs, sweep out the leaves, and put some of the junk in the trash," Nat replied. "I think my goats have been in the barn, when they escaped from their pasture. You know that their pasture is right next to the barn. "

"I'll go tell my mom I'm coming over to help you," said Alex. Nat strolled out to the barn, in no hurry to get started on his chore. He waited for Alex to return from the house next door.

"Goats, have you been in the barn chewing up stuff?" asked Nat. His goats were famous for chewing up anything. Nat remembered the episode of the oldest goat Doc chewing up his coat that Nat's dad had made. Nat's dad had made coats for all the goats the previous winter.

Soon Alex returned. The two boys took inventory of the equipment stored. The old "riding-on" lawn mower needed new tires. The lawn edger stood upright in one corner. An old garden hose stretched in several directions. A garden plow, a hoe, shovels, rakes, and an old rusty wheelbarrow were covered in cobwebs.

"We better use some garden gloves to protect our hands," said Nat. " I would hate to get bitten by a spider or anything else." He and Alex went back toward the house, went into the garage and looked for some garden gloves, which they found on one of the shelves near Nat's dad's workbench. Next, they headed back to the barn storage room to begin their chore.

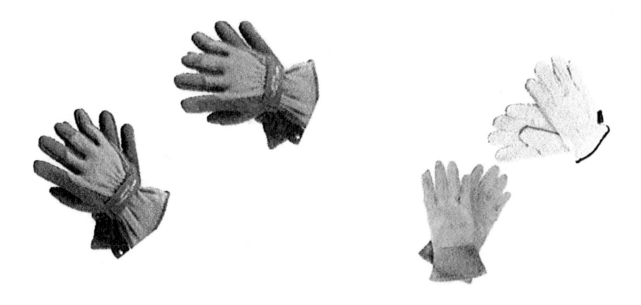

"ooo-ooo-ooo"

"I keep hearing a low moan," said Alex. "What could be causing that sound?

"Maybe it's the wind blowing through a crack in the wall or the roof," said Nat. "I keep thinking it might be some animal caught behind a piece of equipment that we don't see because it is covered with those leaves in the corner or even a ghost or possibly one of our goats. The goats are famous for getting out of their pasture and winding up in some strange place. Let's get to work and see what we can do here."

The boys decided to take out the hoe, the shovels, the rakes, and the old rusty wheelbarrow and laid them on the ground outside on the grass.

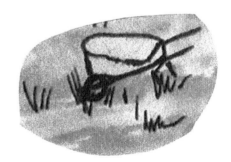

" The 'riding-on' lawn mower will be a challenge to take out of this barn," said Nat. "Alex, if you pull, I will push and the old 'riding on' lawn mower may be willing to move out side on the grass." They pulled and pulled on the old 'riding-on' lawn mower until they had moved it outside to the grass.

The garden hose was more of a challenge as it covered a large area of the floor and twisted in several directions. Nat took the sprayer end of the hose and began to pull it outside toward the grassy area. Alex tried to unwind each of the kinks as Nat pulled on the hose. Some parts of the hose were covered with mounds of leaves that had blown into the storage area.

"Keep pulling, Nat," said Alex. "I think I am about to find the end of this old hose." Finally, after getting all the kinks out and pulling the complete hose out of the storage area, the two boys took a deep breath.

"Whew! That was more of a job than I expected," said Nat. "But that cleared out a nice big area for us to rake."

"ooo-ooo-ooo"

"There goes that sound again," said Alex. " I still cannot figure out where it is coming from. It makes me a little bit scared." The moaning sound continued to intrigue the boys. They knew they needed to struggle with their cleaning job, so they kept on working.

"Our next step is to figure out how to get the garden plow out of here," said Nat. "Alex, if you pull and I push, maybe we can get it to move in the direction we want it to go. So, here we go!" Each boy took this job seriously and each one put his whole strength into moving the garden plow. Finally, after struggling quite a bit, the garden plow began to slowly move in the right direction – the grassy area outside the barn. With so much effort put forth by the two boys, the garden plow arrived on the grassy plot.

" That was a bigger job than I expected," said Nat. "But thanks to you and your strong arms we made that old garden plow do what we wanted it to do."

"ooo-ooo-ooo"

Once again the low moan sounded.

"We cannot let some silly noise stop us from accomplishing our goal for today," said Nat, "Let's decide what to do next. I believe if we make a bar with some nails in it we can hang the rakes, the hoe, the shovel, and possibly the old hose. My dad has some pieces of wood in his shop and a bunch of long nails. I think the hammer is there, too. But first we need to get all the leaves out of the floor of this storage area."

Each boy grabbed a rake. They pulled piles of leaves out of the area and scooped them up with their gloved hands and put the leaves into a bushel basket they found underneath everything. Nat's dad had shown the boys where to deposit the raked leaves. He was making a compost pile of leaves to place around his bushes in the front yard.

After removing three baskets of leaves, the boys could actually see the ground of the storage area.

"Let's clean the cobwebs off the walls next," said Nat. " We are finally seeing the end of this chore. We may be finished before dinner time."

"And don't forget the bar we want to make for the long handled pieces," said Alex. "You take this side wall and I'll take that side wall and we can meet in the middle of the back wall for getting all the cobwebs down. We can just use the rakes to get them off the walls without getting any spiders on us. Just watch for any crawly things. They may turn out to be spiders. "

"ooo-ooo-ooo"

The low moan sounded again.

" I would say we have a ghost in here," said Nat. "As much as we have moved stuff around we would have found the source of the strange noise we are hearing."

"A ghost!" exclaimed Alex. "I really don't believe in ghosts, but this sound sure is a strange one and it really scares me."

After clearing out all the cobwebs, the boys went up to Nat's dad's workshop. They retrieved a board, some nails and the hammer. After it was determined how much space would be needed for two nails to hold each long-handled tool, they began to pound in the nails. Finally they took the board and nailed it to one of the walls on the side. Nat held the board while Alex pounded a nail through the board and into the wall. Then Alex held the board while Nat pounded a nail through the other end of the board and into the wall. They hung the shovel, the hoe, and the rakes each between two nails. They rolled the hose up neatly and placed it over two of the nails.

"ooo-ooo-oo

There goes that low moan again," said Alex. "We have uncovered enough area to prove that we don't have a strange animal caught under anything." The barn storage area was quite improved. The boys were helping each other to accomplish the task that Nat was assigned for the day.

"Look over there on the side of the barn!" exclaimed Nat. "I think that flapping piece of tar paper on the side of the barn is loose enough for the wind to whistle through it. We may have to repair that before we are finished with our job."

" I just hope you are right, because I was really scared." Said Alex. The sound came again.

"ooo-ooo-ooo"

"Here is a slit just big enough for the wind to whistle through and cause the moaning we have heard all morning," said Nat. "Let's go back to Dad's workshop and try to find some fresh tar paper to repair that opening.

The boys went back up to the house and searched around the workshop. They found a small roll of tar-paper they could use to repair the opening on the interior of the barn wall.

They tore a piece off the roll and picked up some short nails. Going back to the barn, they carefully placed the tar- paper over the loose area and nailed it down. They returned the hammer and extra nails back to Nat's dad's workshop.

"You have been a great help, cousin," said Nat. "I could not have done all this without you. Teamwork always makes a job easier. Do you remember when we were on the same Soccer League and we helped each other to score points for our team?"

"I sure do." Said Alex. "Our parents should be very proud of us, too, for working so hard at cleaning out the storage area of your barn. It was not easy. It took a lot of cooperation on our part to get pieces of equipment out of the barn. After we did that, we raked up all those baskets of leaves that covered everything. Then we hauled the baskets of leaves out to your front yard where your dad is making a compost pile for his pretty bushes."

"How would you like to stop for a snack?" said Nat. "I think my mom would be happy to let us have a drink or cookies. I will race you up to the house."

The two boys made a dash toward Nat's house to claim their reward for working hard all morning. They hoped to tell Nat's mom about the ghost in the barn. They wanted tell her exactly how they stopped the strange noise in the barn.

"Mission accomplished," said Nat. The boys were happy that they had solved the mystery of the noise in the barn.

" No more ghosts in this barn," said Nat with a big smile on his face.

Story by Evelyn Heckhaus
Illustrations by Kim Thorn

Printed in the United States
by Baker & Taylor Publisher Services